Acknowledgement

I would like to thank Him for this gift. Thank you also to those who constantly encouraged and believed in me.

Table of Contents

Okra	2
It's What Happens when you are doing Life	3
Wouldn't you rather know?	4
Never Certain	5
Another Year	6
Wall	7
Cryptic	8
Dazed	9
Just For a Few Seconds	12
Only I	13
The Stuff Romance novels are made of…	14
How do we become who we are?	15
Father, Step-Father, Daddy, Dad, Pops, Old Man	16
Porous **Rock**	17
MeTaMorPhoSiS	18
The Hunt	19
Protégée	22
Predator or Prey?	24
The ChaLLenge	26
Aries	29
VIPER RULE	31
Domesticated	33
ReVenge	36
Soursop	38
Hatred	39
The Path	40
Shadows	41
Rose	42
The Dove	43
Friendships	44
Obsession	45
BEAUTY	46

Okra

Sometimes long
Sometimes small
Sometimes soft
Sometimes hard
Hairy from root to tip
A perfect complement to fish
With its slime
and seeds dispersed in a dish
It's a man's thing
because of the appetites it fills
But some women hate
its oozing consistency
while others salivate
over its slipperiness.
Okra,
a tempting,
satisfying
Or detested fruit?

It's What Happens when you are doing Life.

It's waves to surf
Or consume.
It's tornadoes to spin you,
tear you from the roots.
It's an earthquake that tremors
Or obliterates.
It's a sandpit to rise from
Or resist and sink
It's a mud hole to wallow in
And refuse to fight.
It's a confinement to shrink in
Or burst out of as a colossus
It's a death sentence we can't escape
It's the Chair called Life.

Wouldn't you rather know?

Wouldn't you rather know?
Wouldn't it relieve so much anxiety?
Wouldn't it cease the questions?
Wouldn't it make life clear?
Wouldn't it lessen fear?
Wouldn't it make timelines plausible?
Goals achievable?

Wouldn't you rather know?
Wouldn't you rather know?

Never Certain

Carefully laid out path
Methodically planned
Meticulously engineered
Every minute detail
Spontaneity rare
Too many variables
Control
Captain at the helm
Never thrown
Always above water
Or a great diver
Yet
With All precautions
Foundations
Steps
Decisions made
Preventative Actions
Contracts end
Certainty is Frail
Except
Death.

Another Year

New Year brings
The pangs of the previous year sneaking past the 31st
Into the 1st month
Emanating
Fear of the unknown
Anxiety
Panic
Failures to contend with
Wonders of the losses to come
The new issues
The new age
The new expenses
The new aims
Targets to hit
Goals to surpass
As the New Year tries to shed the old
But it creeps and seeps
Lingers like a shadow
Until you give in, endure till
The end of another year.

Wall

Criticisms, Criticisms
The wall hears
muffled sobs
The wall sees,
Struggles, trials
The wall faces her from all directions
Unable to enclose
The wall embraces her back when thrust upon it
The wall stops her falls
Her wall defends
Stands its ground
Yet no comfort
Only distance
Yet no warmth
Only cold, smooth texture-
cracks embedded,
plastered over
and coated
Her wall.

Cryptic

Never straightforward
Never plain
Shades of grey rear its head
Why?
Why not yes or no
But
Yet,
It's complicated
Maybe
A cryptic message undecipherable
From the brightening of the horizon to the darkening
Codes
Formulas
Questions
Everywhere.

Dazed

Hazy, blurred, half-conscious
That's what's called to mind
When I think of that night.

A routine 'no cooking day'
Clouds grey
Pregnant with showers
An urge, yearning for chicken
Takes me miles from home.

The scintillating aroma
Satisfaction felt when the craving was fed
Made my journey worthwhile
Raging rain, thunder and lightning proclaimed
A warning
But
All in vain

Home once more,
A tornado brewed in my depths
Expelled through the usual orifices
An ache, the pounding sound
of ten thousand jack-hammers in my head
Refuge, sought on the plush, soft bed
As I curled comma style

Watching myself shaken awake
Panic in the eyes of loved ones
The contents of my grown belly poking,
Frantic with movements
Carried to the vehicle,
Eyes rolling to the back of my head
Body convulsing
Tongue chewed on like a tasty meal

Hearing my name called,
From a distance, I slowly inhabited my body
With eyes confused, annoyed at being awoken from a dream,
From sleep on the plush soft bed
Where I curled comma style.

Conscious, I see concern in the faces of
My doctor and loved ones
Then
The interrogation began
What did I recall?
All while being transported from one hospital
to a prepped surgery room in another
a few minutes later
speech leaves my mouth and again I'm drawn into
unconsciousness

A bright light and semblance of a face
Emerged over me
A mask placed on my face
Then
Unconsciousness

Dazed, struggling to awake,
I spy a sterile room
Beds adorned with white sheets
The poignant smell of disinfectant
A semi flagpole machine attached to my wrist
Through a tube
The same wrist tagged and prodded with a needle
A bag of liquid forced intravenously
Pain from a horizontal wound at my V-line,
Another tube inserted into yet another orifice
Collected urine

All these foreign to me

Yet,
The one foreign body that had
grown in me, attached, nourished
was nowhere
insight

Faintly I uttered the words
To the new uniformed attraction to the room
She left
Hope sprung
She returned
A bundle was handed over
Warm to the touch, I held, inspected tiny appendages,
Closed eyes, hairy scalp
Everything, Perfect
Except
No Breath.

Just For a Few Seconds

Just for a few seconds
Under the loving gaze of your Mom
Did she hold you, imagine, cry
Experience the joy of motherhood if just for a few seconds.

Only I

Only I have a void
Only I feel left out
Only I shed tears
Only I mourn; yearn
Only I have been scared
Only I lie awake in these rowed quarters listening to screams
Only I have no joy to share
Only I have visitors search for the right words of comfort to share
Only I search for sanity amidst celebrations
Only I am restless at night, tainted in my sleep
Only I remember a still body
Only I receive flowers of condolences instead of congratulations
Only I have rock hard breasts that drain white liquid
It is only I among these nurturing mothers that have no young to suckle.

The Stuff Romance novels are made of…

Young and impressionable,
Hungry like a worm weaving through frivolous romance novels, the occasional teen crime fiction and suspense,
But the favourites were Austin, Bronte and Hardy
Proper damsels awaiting the proverbial knight in armour

It is no surprise that I envisioned the perfect gentleman to be the one,
The one to deflower me, wed me, live happily ever after with me.

Diverse mixing of eras -music, fashion, movies- thwarted the prince and white horse
For brightly coloured cars and "bad"boys.

Yet a blend was what I sought,
The "bad" boy exterior with a genteel man's heart
So enthralled was I with this vision
That I projected unto
A dark knight
And yearned for him.

Fate brought to bear the maiden and this 'knight'
Only the rules of the classics did not exist

He did not rescue me, wed me, live happily ever after with me
after deflowering me

Instead I was plucked, placed on display
Til the newness faded and I began to wither
Conquered not rescued
Off he rode to another garden

Deceived, betrayed by a concoction of time periods and ideals
Wishing to invent the perfect dichotomy
Led to my first lesson of seeing
the fluff romance novels are made of.

How do we become who we are?

How do we become who we are?
From birth do things come innate?
Do we mimic and reciprocate parents/guardians?
Do we read emotions and do accordingly?
In fear of a reaction, do we lie to escape consequences?
Does absenteeism or loss mold us; enslave us?

How do we become who we are?
Does religion make us cynics and skeptics because we can't
Deal with or explain loss, cruelty, pain and suffering?
Do we become recluse, envious and intolerant when others' path spring instead of winter?
Do people need to tread lightly around us for fear of crushing the egg shells laid out?

How do we become who we are?
Do we respect others point of view?
Do we empathize with others and not flaunt good fortune?
Do we have concepts of not only good vs. bad, right vs. wrong
But a middle ground?
Do people keep leaving our lives, detaching, uprooting foundations
That we chalk it up to 'it's them not me'?
Can so many people be wrong?

How do we become who we are?
Do people fear being honest around us?
Do we breed contempt for others due to circumstances, possessions, lifestyle
Not knowing how that grass got so green?
Do we genuinely love and care for others or are we self serving at the expense of others?

How do we become who we are?
And
Do we want to change who we have become?

Father, Step-Father, Daddy, Dad, Pops, Old Man

Father, Step-Father, Daddy, Dad, Pops, Old man;
All names given to the male figure in our lives,
whether biological, as a replacement or adoptive,
All names connote different meanings
but all are donors.

Any male can be a donor but not many can be called DAD.

Dad, Daddy, Pops, Old man, you are more than a Father
You are strength, understanding, love, affection.
You are a light in my world, my role-model.
You have nurtured me, guarded me, and lead me into the world.

I know I may have been disappointing once or twice,
I know I may have made you proud,
But no matter which you stood by me, encouraged me
and made me proud to call YOU
Dad.

Our candid, comic, caring moments are many, and all treasured.
I see the sacrifices you have made, continue to make and all are
appreciated.
Your bright smile, affectionate chuckle and
even the late night 'cherry' tone/laughter
have given my life joy.

Pops, thank you for helping to bring me into this world,
Thank you for choosing to be a Daddy.
And when you have become my Old man, you will still be
More than a Father, you will be the man who lives for his children.

Porous **Rock**

Can't express without fear of loss
Walking cautiously like in a minefield
Always on guard
Every word, action carefully chosen
Or it comes tumbling down.
Years of knowledge seem like only days
Fragile instead of sturdy
Energy and Effort exerted; yet the
Yield is never two-fold.
Never regretted but it drains
Delight is taken in being the rock
But as turgid as it is, it needs support
Tiny holes within widen bit by bit with each silent hurt
Breaking away the layers.
Exposed,
Strength dwindling,
It needs
And
Yearns too.

MeTaMorPhoSiS

Joint decision
Mutual Bliss
Exploration…Contact
Minute transformations
Unknown Growth
Transparent Form
Symbiotic living
Physical effects
      Movements
Contentment

Then,
Convulsions
Invasion
Forcible removal
Fleeting Hope
Last breath

Now,
Cocooned
Questions, Doubt
Physical reversals
Fear, Pain

Future,
Stasis, or Butterfly?

The Hunt

Leo, the lion of the jungle

had keen instincts,

he knew the jungle well,

was versed in the game and a worthy adversary.

He caught my eye when my pack was lying about the field.

His light brown coat glistened in the sun,

his eyes were stunning hazel

but what drew my gaze was that this lion had no mane,

he was bald.

Yet he did not receive ridicule

but was gazed upon by his pride with admiration from his courage.

Leo, became my obsession

My first Alpha confrontation.

I approached him direct steering into his eyes,

making my slow, sensual walk speak for me.

I let off pheromones and watched him

indulge in the sweet aroma of me.

Standing directly in front of him

I ran my tongue around his whiskers, then his mouth

and tried to enter his sanctuary.

He pulled back,

glared at me through that hazel heaven,

parted his mouth in a curious smirk and reproached my kiss.

My world shattered as he shook his head in disapproval.

Here I had built up in my mind that I was a diva,

queen of the game and now

I was being critiqued by a veteran.

With bended head, I tucked my tail between my legs and began to walk

away.

He outstretched his limb and blocked my path.

He steered into my depths,

blew a lash from my eye;

a breath which sent shivers down my spine,

my limbs and

rested just between my legs.

Already his touch, eyes and breath had me undone,

and I thought, I have no power,

I know nothing of this game;

I am innocent.

My inside exploded once his tongue licked my mouth,

At once he awaked the dark desire within me ,

bringing fireworks to the once dormant cave.

Leo at that moment not only gained my love but respect.

He became the master and I,

the grasshopper.

I watched him,

learned from him,

adored and admired him,

while he imparted forbidden secrets of the jungle.

Secrets that will one day save my life.

Protégée

In time Leo, my master,

tried to use his knowledge of the game

to redirect my affection,

but instead was himself caught by the allure of me,

his student.

Leo and I connected but never indulged in that sacred bond.

Instead we became great comrades, with mutual respect and shared love.

With my masters' theories being put into practice,

I was unstoppable;

a queen in every right;

long midnight flowing hair,

defined shapely legs,

handcrafted curves,

and a well sculpted face.

Smooth, sleek, demure was my stride,

my gaze seductive,

eyes of depth, dreamy, daring,

lips light pink with shades of dark brown,

to match my dark complexion.

Panther, a leopard whose coat shows no spots,

my blemishes hidden within.

Predator or Prey?

Animal urges, primal instincts, pheromones fueling my desire;

all these images cloud my mind on a daily basis.

The constant hunt, battle, is what I live for.

I am Panther, the huntress of the jungle.

Since a cub, I urged to be different

to explore, to deviate,

but in my pack, deviations were forbidden.

I grew to learn how to conceal my animalistic nature,

my urge for flesh, contact and appeared to be normal.

Silently, outside the confines of my dwelling,

I experimented, hunted, conquered and I grew to love

the rush, the game, the hunt.

There I was a beauty, a divine creation living life,

carefree, adventurous, on the edge,

and most importantly in secret.

We all know that fate, the Gods, density,

whatever cosmic being you believe in,

had to provide me with a test; an obstacle;

a hunt to keep me humble;

to bring me back down to earth;

to tame me if you will.

Unbeknownst to me.

The ChaLLenge

In my eighteenth year of glory,

There came along Viper;

he was my mirror image,

the hunter, my King.

We were the same yet different.

I stalked him from a distance,

watching his graceful slide, his flagpole stature,

admiring his seductive sizzle,

swimming in his hypnotic gaze,

waiting to make my move.

Studying his hunting grounds

I presented myself as a wounded prey,

and waited for Viper to strike.

I watched as he hesitantly glimpsed at me,

tasting my pheromones with his tongue,

sliding cautiously towards me on his guard as any true hunter.

There I laid, a seemingly helpless prey,

playing the game to bait *my* prey.

Viper finally confronted me,

gazed into my dark brown eyes,

encircled me with his strong slender body and whispered

sensitive, sensational, sensual, sentiments in my ear,

kissed my unseen wounds with his mouth slow and fearlessly.

I was weak,

for his grasp on me both physically and emotionally was unrelenting.

So enthralled was I that instead of fighting,

instead of utilizing the lessons of my master,

instead of trapping my prey,

he caught *me* and therein started the bound,

Viper had on me.

A bondage that lasted for what seemed like a lifetime,

I became domesticated,

no longer was I Panther but a mere Cat.

I no longer hunted, in secret or otherwise,

I was *tamed*.

Living the life in the shadow of Viper,

no longer shining on my own,

my diva star dimming with every control, power he took.

Tamed, I was, yet Viper was gaining glory in the game.

He conquered prey after prey in secret

but I knew the smell of the hunt,

knew the glow it gave the Ego,

knew the scent of victory.

I watched from the sideline, me, his trophy,

mounted on a pedestal, disillusioned to think happy.

Bound to Viper drew me back to a place of darkness,

back to my youth, a feeling of helplessness

back to the time of Aries.

Aries

A distant leader of our pack,

the pretender,

the predator;

Instead of hunting for the pack,

his game was within the pack.

Aries, the amiable pack leader;

all the cubs were drawn to him.

He was youthful, exuberant and sly.

He watched my siblings and me grow,

being nurtured, groomed, and scolded.

But I was the most mature and as such he set his sights

on the upcoming, zealous, silky coated, shapely Panther.

He came disguised as a confidant,

one to lay all growing pains on.

Instead he saw his opening, my unguarded wall and leaped over.

Before any inclination of the hunt or game

I was taught how to be a prey;

to lie still while being sniffed, prodded, tasted and salivated over.

I learned to be helpless, to keep secrets, to bleed.

This lesson I learned from Aries.

Youthful zeal became

cautious,

defensive,

aggressive

instincts.

Aries saw the fangs of Panther

the second time he tried to school,

he now glares from a far,

mingling in the pack, watching, waiting to leap over again.

VIPER RULE

Once again, now

defenseless,

with my guard down,

wrapped up by Viper, his venom coursing through my veins.

Trapped…

Panther screamed to be released from within.

Her methodic nature brewed slowly within.

She began to plan her escape

from an infatuated filled dwelling where Viper ruled;

did as he pleased in the jungle,

while Cat was housed,

bowing in a servitude manner to his every whim.

It seemed as if she would never regain control.

Dually she still lived with her pack,

was still a cub in her parents' eyes,

still living a secret life;

a double life that began to take a toll.

Cat, the oldest cub, well schooled,

role-model for her siblings,

the embodiment of her parents' dreams,

aspirations and goals versus

Panther, the untamed,

spotted,

aggressive,

defensive alter.

Viper cared for Panther in his way;

But he was just never any good at reciprocating feelings.

Why would he be?

He is of a cold-blooded family, his nature.

Panther, however, was a warm blooded mammal

whose pack was protective and caring

so she yearned for that affection.

The realization dawned that Viper could never

shed his cold blooded layers,

or be of her nature

that they would always be bound by

the hunt; the game, because they were predators at heart.

Domesticated

Realizing the inevitability, Panther,

day after day became stronger,

while Cat shrunk into the unconscious.

The journey was mountainous,

Viper was not about to release his fangs from his prized possession,

but one step at a time Panther denied her heart

and turned to her defenses.

Relapses did occur, as with any drug

and Viper's venom was no different.

Occasionally Cat emerged, frail, weeping, and suicidal,

not only due to Viper's actions

but her past

her double existence.

Thoughts of sweet, serene sleep crept to mind

taunted with strings from each direction.

Not knowing what path to take,

I chased all in an effort to catch one,

proving futile.

left drained.

An inkling of control sneaked into the mind.

Decide when to or live in fear of the unknown?

Inside the dwelling,

isolated,

Cat circled the space for a comfortable spot and sat,

licked her limb and positioned it over a won prey carcass

Eyes gripped tight, heart pumping, veins pulsating,

thoughts traveling at the speed of light;

slowly Cat lowered her limb to the blade.

With conviction, limb rested on the blade

In a back and forth motion,

then Panther whispered from deep within,

"Don't let them win."

the twinge of the blade already giving a slight pain,

the whisper came again slightly louder,

"Don't let them win."

A trickle of blood dropped on the ground.

This time, Panther was clear and firm,

"Don't let them win!"

With raised limb from the blade, licking her wound

Panther emerged from the cave with determination in her eyes and stride.

ReVenge

Bravely stalking Viper's lair

steadfast in ending this parasitic relationship

Viper had just shed his clothing

was beaming with newness;

his slender figure tempting;

his aroma bewitching.

Panther felt Cat tremble,

sending goose bumps down her loins.

Panther closed her eyes, swallowed hard

willed Cat back into her sub-consciousness.

Viper sizzled, "Come here kitty Cat."

"Come, let me devour you."

Panther, once again, closed her eyes,

took two deep relaxing breaths and in a sturdy voice,

roared, "NO!"

He slithered over to her and began to encircle her,

ignoring her outburst.

Panther stood her ground,

looked in his bewitching, hypnotic eyes

"Your venom no longer poisons my veins.

I am immune to your charms."

And with that she sank her teeth into his skin

and pulled

leaving him,

exposed,

skin shed.

He slithered on his belly towards her

Sizzling his silvery forked tongue

But she kept her eyes forward

New horizons beaconed

Victory was hers

She now controlled

She was the snake charmer

and she reveled in it.

Soursop

Not the most attractive,
But fleshy and tender on the inside.
Milky juices flow
When fingers prod the meat
Of the fruit
Leaving imprints.
Seeds from deep within
Travel to the centre of the fruit
To be fertilized-
Grow saplings
But more often than not
They are sucked from the fruit-
Wasted.

Hatred

A gully,
A deep void
Enveloped in darkness
Wrapped tightly with slithering creatures
Water
Rising
Fear
A Gasp
Then, grasping at thin air
Sinking ever so slowly into eternity.

The Path

A set trail
unlikely travelled
rocky, narrow, tricky terrain

The skilled traveler walking
with the anchor of the world
trips, falls, hungers, thirsts.
He now walks with unsure footing,
trying to balance.
He is burdened as the load diminishes him.
He is fearful.
He retreats.

The wise traveler,
walks bare
steps freely, surely.
His walk is fixed,
no need to balance like on a beam
because he is not alone.

Shadows

Blank darkness
Loneliness
Floating thoughts
Haunting images
Racing heart beat
Then light, a hand
      progression
clouds drift
far skies peek through
      regeneration
purpose
hope
shadows still lurk
but dear not step into the
light
the light progresses
eliminating the shadows
with each step.

Rose

On a bleak and foggy morn
In a place with beauty rare
A sweet scent fills the air
And there in the middle of thorny green
A single rose stood tall and lean.

The dew falls on petals so soft
Like the skin of a newborn being
Then a ray of light appears
And sits on green hills do fair
Giving the rose a wonderful glare.

The Dove

I once knew a dove, so handsome and smart
He touched my heart with its gentle wing,
so smooth and soft.
I grew to love and treasure my heavenly dove
Who's life was a mystery.
His understanding and my daily care
of his broken part, filled me with purpose
and made me soar through clouds of love
with wings filled with trust.

But now it's time for him to fly,
As the old saying goes,
"If you love something set it free,
and if it comes back to you, it's meant to be."
So into a world of opportunity it flew
While I sat and wondered on what could or should
Be.

Friendships

Friendships are like flowers;
It blossoms in favorable conditions
and withers in stagnant, infertile soil.
But it always grows with time and care.

Friendships are like bridges;
It connects and separates.
Each end may be different
Each end may lead to another path
But meeting half way is half the journey

Friendships are like the ocean;
Dangerous, with violent waves
That brew a storm.
But it can be calm and serene;
perfect for sailing on by.

Obsession

Obsession is nothing but a thorny bush
It pricks,
And scrapes,
And competes,
And spreads to places on the earth –
Smothering others.
All the time
It's been growing in the dark
And reaching new heights.
So you need to turn away
Don't neglect to prune
Cause you envision a rose
Don't succumb –
There is a way out
Over the hedge
Don't fall in
Rise above the thorny bush.

BEAUTY

In all the cluster, confusion of wildness, shapes and sizes,
flashing lights of shades and colors peek my every interest.
Focused on a feeling deep within that your beauty is far from the rest
Hesitation grows, but the will of regret is even greater.
This I must put to the test;
I engage in a dance of words to set your mind at ease.
Strutting myself, to show you that I'm better than them.
I can even do it with a little tenderness…

Made in the USA
Columbia, SC
04 August 2022